PUSS IN BOOTS

There once lived a miller who had three sons. The miller was very old and he knew that he was dying so he gathered his sons together.

"Sons, you know I am poor, so I'm afraid I have very little to leave you when I die," he said. "To my eldest son, I leave the mill, to my middle son I leave my donkey and to my youngest son I only have my cat to give, but I also have a few gold coins, so you can have those too."

Soon after, he died, leaving his sons to make the most of the things their father had given them.

The youngest son was too poor to even feed his cat.
"Don't worry, all I need is a pair of boots and a sack and I will make you a wealthy man," said the cat.
So, with the coins that the miller had left him, the young man bought his cat a pair of new boots. He then called at his brother's mill for a corn sack.

This book belongs to:

....

PUBLISHED BY PETER HADDOCK LIMITED,
BRIDLINGTON, ENGLAND
PRINTED IN ITALY

ISBN O 7105 0380 6

The cat was very proud of his new boots and set out at once to keep his promise to his master. He picked some carrots from a nearby field and laid them inside the corn sack to which he had attached a rope. The rope was looped over a tree branch and the cat hid behind the tree with the end of the rope in his paw. By and by, along came an unsuspecting rabbit who was tempted by the smell of the carrots and into the sack it went, then, the clever cat pulled the rope.

Next the cat set off to walk to the palace with the fine rabbit in the sack over his shoulder. It took the cat almost a day to get there but eventually he arrived at the palace steps.

The cat knew exactly what to do and he marched in and asked to see the King.

The King was a kindly man and said of course he would see the cat who could talk, although he was very surprised as it wasn't every day he met a talking cat! The cat walked briskly up the red carpet to the King who was seated on his throne.

"Please accept this gift from the Marquis of Carrabas," said the cat, who bowed low and offered the rabbit.

"Would you thank your master very much," replied the King, who was amused by the cat with the boots.

The next day the cat repeated his trick with the corn sack and the rope. This time, he had placed a little corn inside and a pheasant strolled into the sack, casually pecking at the corn. The next thing it knew, it was hanging upside down in the sack in mid air!

The cat trotted off to the palace with the gift for the King who was again delighted and told the cat to thank the "Marquis of Carrabas" although he dare not admit that he had never heard of him.

Later that week the cat returned to his master and told him to go with him to the river not far from the palace. The miller's son was puzzled but all the same he did as he was told.

When they reached the river, the cat told his master to jump into the river and to pretend to be drowning when the King's coach came close.

"Stop, stop, please help! My master, the Marquis of Carrabas, is drowning," shouted the cat as the King's coach came past.

Immediately, the King told his guardsmen to rescue the cat's master.

"Some thief has stolen his clothes, he left them here when he went to swim," said the cat to the King.

"We'll soon find him some more," said the King and gave the cat a large rug to wrap round the miller's son.

They were both invited to the palace for a hot meal.

While the King, his daughter and the miller's son were settling into the carriage, the cat ran to a nearby field where some labourers and the servants were helping to harvest the corn.

"When the coach comes past, would you shout *'hurray for the Marquis of Carrabas'* and, if the King stops, tell him that all the fields belong to the Marquis," said the cat and he gave them a gold coin.

The labourers were rather simple and did as the cat had told them. When the King heard them shout, he stopped the coach to talk to them. He was most impressed when he was told that the "Marquis" owned all the fields. He was beginning to think that this Marquis could well be a good suitor for his daughter, the Princess.

The fields, in fact, belonged to a wicked wizard who lived in a large castle at the top of a hill. The cat decided it was time he paid this wizard a visit and set off as soon as he and the young man left the palace.

The cat knocked on the castle's huge front door. The wicked wizard opened it and was surprised to see a cat with boots on. Puss told the wizard that he had heard that he could cast many clever spells and he had come to find out if this was true.
The wizard let him into the castle and started to show the cat
what kind of spells he could do.
"I am told you can turn into any animal you like," said Puss.
Immediately, the wizard turned into a huge lion which startled the poor cat.
The wizard at once turned back into his ordinary self.
"That is easy,"said the cat. "But can you turn yourself into something tiny?"
"Of course I can," replied the wizard.
"I bet you couldn't turn yourself into a mouse," said Puss in Boots.

As quick as lightning the wizard cast a spell and just as quickly, the clever cat pounced on the mouse and ate it up.

The King had been invited by the cat to come to the Marquis's castle. The miller's son had a fine home with servants who readily agreed to serve their new master, the wizard had not been well-liked at all. The young man's servants and cooks helped to organise a lavish banquet in honour of the King and the Princess. Later that evening, the guests arrived and the Marquis of Carrabas greeted them. When the Princess arrived, the Marquis thought how beautiful she was and he decided to ask her to marry him now that he was a rich man.

The King had decided that the young man was ideal to be his daughter's husband and hoped he would ask her to marry him. He decided that he would make him a Prince and he asked for his sword. The Marquis knelt before the king and he was made a Prince.

Then the dancing commenced now that the feast had been eaten and everyone enjoyed themselves.

As the Prince and the Princess were dancing together, the cat heard the Prince ask the beautiful girl to marry him. He also heard the Princess's reply which, of course, was "yes."

The cat had kept his promise to his master. Not only was he a Prince and very wealthy, but he was also very happy. As his reward, the cat lived in luxury for the rest of his days.

THE END